Cindy Ellen
A WILD WESTERN CINDERELLA

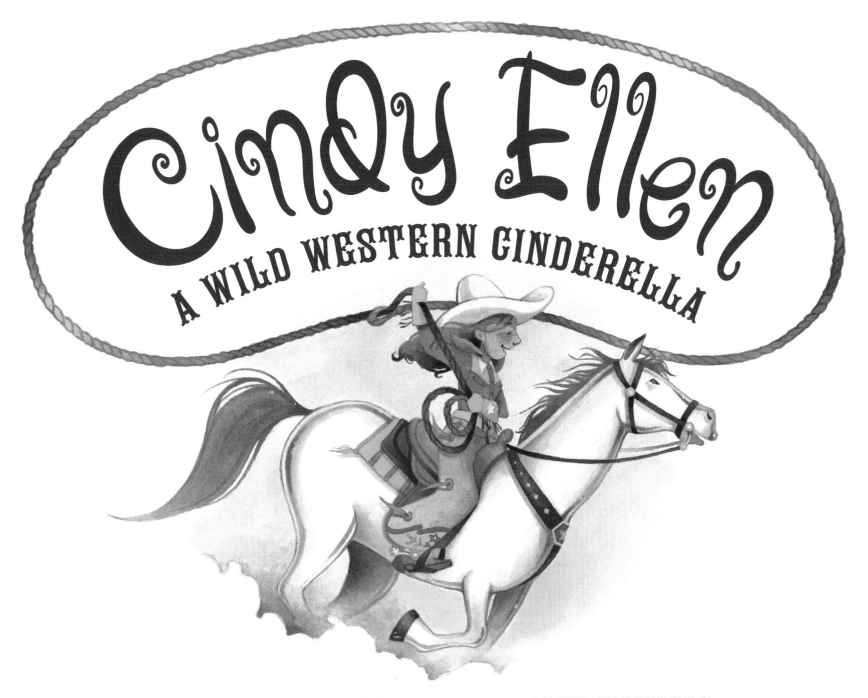

by SUSAN LOWELL × illustrated by JANE MANNING

JOANNA COTLER BOOKS
An Imprint of HarperCollinsPublishers

Cindy Ellen: *A Wild Western Cinderella*
Text copyright © 2000 by Susan Lowell
Illustrations copyright © 2000 by Jane Manning
Printed in the U.S.A. All rights reserved.
http://www.harperchildrens.com

Library of Congress Cataloging-in-Publication Data
Lowell, Susan, 1950–
   Cindy Ellen : a wild western Cinderella / by Susan Lowell ; illustrated by Jane Manning.
      p.   cm.
   "Joanna Cotler books."
   Summary: Cindy Ellen loses one of her diamond spurs at the square dance in this wild western
retelling of the classic Cinderella story.
   ISBN 0-06-027446-8. — ISBN 0-06-027447-6 (lib. bdg.)
   [1. Fairy tales.   2. Folklore—France.]   I. Manning, Jane K., ill.   II. Cinderella. English.
III. Title.
PZ8.L9485Ci   2000   99-21194
[398.2]—dc21   CIP

Typography by Alicia Mikles
1   2   3   4   5   6   7   8   9   10
❖
First Edition

For Ilona Vukovic-Gay, who makes magic music.
—S.L.

To Bob.
—J.M.

ONCE THERE WAS a rancher who married for his second wife the orneriest woman west of the Mississippi. She was meaner than a rattlesnake, and she had two daughters who were the spitting image of her. The rancher also had a daughter, who was just as sweet and gentle as she could be. Her name was Cindy Ellen.

Cindy was a pretty good cowgirl, too. Riding her little gray horse, she wrangled and roped and galloped and loped with the best buckaroos on the range.

But as soon as the wedding was over, that snaky old stepmother began to pick on poor Cindy Ellen. She was so good she made her stepsisters look bad. So her stepmother made her do all the dirty work around the ranch.

"Mend those fences! Tend those cows!" she would yell. "And shovel out that corral!"

The stepsisters never did a lick of work all day, but Cindy didn't dare complain to her daddy because his new wife wore the pants in the family.

When her chores were done, the poor girl used to sit down and rest among the ashes and cinders at the edge of the fireplace, so her older stepsister nicknamed her "Cinderbottom." The younger sister called her "Sanderella." But underneath her dirty old clothes, Cindy Ellen was still as pretty as a peach.

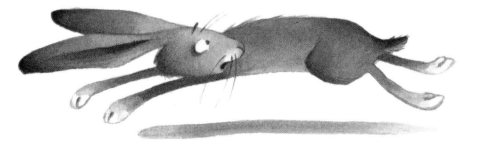

Then one day the biggest cattle king for miles around invited all his neighbors to a two-day celebration, first a wild and woolly rodeo, and then a square dance— a real Western fandango!

Cindy's stepsisters puffed up like two turkey gobblers. Even though they couldn't ride, they decided to gussy themselves up fit to kill and enter the rodeo. Nice, patient Cindy Ellen ironed their frilly shirts and frizzed their hair for them.

"Don't you wish you could go too, Cinderbottom?" sneered the older sister.

"Aw, you're just poking fun at me," said Cindy sadly.

"You're right," laughed the younger sister. "Nobody could tell *you* from a cloud of dust, Sanderella."

As soon as they were gone, poor Cindy Ellen broke down and cried. Then suddenly she heard a noise outside, almost like gunfire . . . but not quite. It wasn't BANG BANG! It was more like BING BING! And there stood a little old lady with a golden pistol still smoking in her hand.

"Who are you?" gasped Cindy Ellen.

"Say hello to your fairy godmother, sugarfoot," the old lady said. She twirled the pistol, slapped it back into its holster, and took a good hard look at Cindy. "What's the matter with you, honey? You're as down and dirty as a flop-eared hound dog. Stand up straight! Dust yourself off!"

"I want to go to the rodeo," sobbed Cindy Ellen. "Can you help?"

"Maybe *sí*, maybe no," said her fairy godmother. "Magic is plumb worthless without gumption. What you need first, gal, is some gravel in your gizzard. Grit! Guts! Stop that tomfool blubbering, and let's get busy. Time's a-wastin'."

She reached for her golden six-gun, and Cindy yelled, "Don't shoot!"

But her godmother had already fired . . . straight up in the air.

BING! PING!

Glittery sparkles floated down from the sky and sprinkled Cindy all over with fairy dust. Instantly her heart was filled with strength and happiness, and her rags turned into the finest riding clothes west of the East.

A creamy white Stetson hat crowned her shining hair, golden buckskin chaps encircled her legs, and a pretty little pair of cowboy boots hugged her feet like gloves. Buckled to the heel of each boot was a spur that shot out rays of fiery light. Those spurs were set with diamonds as big as sugar lumps!

"Now," said her fairy godmother briskly, "where's that horse of yours?"

She fired her magic pistol into the air— *ZING!*—and Cindy's little gray horse

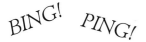

became a little silver horse with a softly sparkling coat. His hoofs glittered as he pawed the ground.

"Hit the trail, honey!" the old lady said. "Remember, there ain't no horse that can't be rode, and there ain't no man that can't be throwed! And one more thing. Get home by midnight, gal, or you'll be sorr-ee!"

When Cindy Ellen pulled up at the rodeo, everybody turned and stared at the dazzling stranger on the silver horse. The rich rancher's son, a rodeo champion by the name of Joe Prince, came forward wearing the biggest belt buckle you ever saw, and swept his hat off his head.

"Pleased to meet you, ma'am!" he said.

"Likewise," said Cindy.

Just then, Cindy's older stepsister rode a bucking bronco into the arena, and before she could say "oopsy daisy," that cayuse wrinkled his spine, boiled over, and sent her chasing clouds way up in the sky. Then she bit the dust.

Next came the second stepsister, but she couldn't ride a rail fence in a stiff breeze, and pretty soon she was eating gravel just like her sister.

Cindy Ellen helped her stepsisters up and brushed them off, but they never even recognized her. Then she remembered her godmother's gift of gumption, and she gave Joe Prince a big daredevil grin.

"My turn!" said Cindy Ellen.

Cindy Ellen climbed aboard a salty bronc with a bellyful of bedsprings, a real rip-snorter. She touched him with her diamond spurs, and first he tried to crow-hop, and then he catbacked, and he sunfished, and he windmilled, and he jacknifed, but Cindy stuck to the saddle like a postage stamp.

"Ride 'em, cowgirl!" cried the crowd, and Cindy Ellen was the winner, with every curl in place.

Next, with a figure eight, a butterfly, and a wedding ring, she won the trick roping event. And then she and her little horse really burned the breeze. They kicked the jackrabbits right off the trail. They left their shadows twenty miles behind them. And they won the horse race. They even beat Joe Prince!

But Joe didn't seem to care. He rode herd on Cindy Ellen right up to a quarter of twelve at night, when she suddenly recalled her godmother's warning and went galloping home.

By the time she got there, her fine duds had shriveled into sorry rags again, but she still had plenty of gumption. After a while, her stepsisters hobbled in, all stove-up from the rodeo.

"Ha, ha, you missed the champion cowgirl!" the older sister jeered. "Nobody knows her name, or where she disappeared to."

"And that ol' Joe Prince is eating his heart out!" said the younger one.

"I bet she comes to the square dance tomorrow night," said Cindy, with her new daredevil grin.

The next evening her stepsisters got all dressed up like a sore thumb and strutted away to the dance, leaving Cindy Ellen all alone. But not for long.

"What's that?" she said, peeking out the window.

It looked like a cross between a comet and a dust storm. It sounded like silver bells mixed with dynamite.

"Let's get crackin', sweet pea," shouted her fairy godmother. "You're late! Rustle me up the biggest, dustiest, lumpiest squash you can find."

And . . . Z-Z-ZINGO! . . . the squash became a stagecoach.

"Next, we check the trap line," said her godmother.

Quick as a wink, she turned six cactus mice into six dappled horses, a fat pack rat into a stagecoach driver, and a rough, tough horned toad into a stagecoach guard, riding shotgun beside the driver.

"But what about my ugly old clothes?" asked Cindy.

The old lady answered with a blast of fairy dust that melted into a dress that shone like the sun, the moon, and all the stars together. The skirt floated over petticoats as soft and puffy as summer clouds. A rainbow of jewels glowed around Cindy Ellen's neck, and the little diamond spurs sparkled once more upon her boot heels.

"Thank you, ma'am!" she cried.

The fairy godmother blew the smoke from her pistol, holstered it, and dusted off her hands.

"Remember, Miss Cindy, pretty is as pretty does," she said. "Magic can backfire. Midnight or bust!"

Cindy promised, and the stagecoach rumbled away.

When Cindy Ellen arrived at the cattle king's square dance, the fiddlers were tuning up for a toe-tapping jamboree. Joe Prince reached for Cindy's hand the instant he laid eyes on her.

"Buckle on your partners, folks," he called. "And tell 'em to hang on! Let's shake our hoofs like lightning until the early dawn!"

And Cindy answered: "Hurry up, cowboy, don't be slow. Allemande left and do-si-do!"

Hand over hand and heel over heel, Joe and Cindy danced the daisy chain, the whirlaway, the curlicue, and the grand sashay. They made their feet go *whickety-whack*!

"Swing 'em, boys," cried Cindy, "and do it right!"

And Joe called back: "Swing those girls till the middle of the night!"

Twirling, swirling, Cindy Ellen lost track of time, until all at once she heard the clock begin to strike twelve. She hightailed it out of there lickety-split!

"Whoa!" yelled Joe, hot on her heels, but he couldn't catch her. One of the diamond spurs fell off Cindy's boot as she ran, though, and Joe picked it up carefully out of the dust.

Meanwhile back at the ranch, not a particle remained of Cindy's gorgeous outfit, except for the second diamond spur, which she tucked away in her hip pocket.

Pretty soon word got out that the champion cowgirl was a wanted woman. She'd left Joe Prince so lovelorn that he was tracking her throughout the territory, and he vowed to marry the horsewoman whose boot fitted the little diamond spur. He tried it on many a foot, but not one could wear it.

At last he came riding up to Cindy's father's place.

"Go shovel out the stable!" hissed the stepmother, and Cindy reluctantly obeyed.

First Joe tried the diamond spur on the younger stepsister, but no matter how he stretched the straps, her hoof was too big. The older sister had crushed her feet into little bitty boots, so just for an instant the spur almost fitted. But then her boot split open, and her toes popped out like puppies from a basket, and Joe Prince muttered "Sorry," and headed for the door.

"My turn," said a voice that stopped him in his tracks.

It was Cindy Ellen. And although her mean stepsisters almost died laughing, Joe let Cindy have her chance, fair and square, and when he put the diamond spur around her dirty little boot it fitted perfectly.

Then she pulled out the second diamond spur and buckled it onto her other boot. And at that very moment Cindy's little horse gave a whinny, and everyone heard a noise like . . .

WHINGO! WHANGO! KA-ZING!

"Let 'er rip!" shouted Cindy Ellen's fairy godmother, brandishing her golden pistol.

"Hold your fire!" yelled Joe Prince.

But glistening sparks of fairy dust were already sprinkling down everywhere. They turned Cindy's clothes from cotton to satin, and they put quite a twinkle in Joe's eye. And Cindy's horse began to sparkle.

"Yee haw!" yelled the fairy godmother.

So Cindy Ellen and Joe Prince got hitched and lived happily ever after in a ranch house full of love and rodeo trophies. Cindy's family moved to town, where both stepsisters married city slickers. And Cindy's little horse kept his sparkling coat and his glittering hoofs to the end of his days.

A LITTLE WESTERN LORE

The true story of the West includes many cowgirls as well as cowboys. Just as they did long ago, ranch girls and boys still learn to ride, rope, and tend their animals, especially at roundups. The Spanish word for "roundup" is *rodeo*: originally, a time in the Old West when neighboring ranchers gathered and sorted their cattle. Then when the work was done, they ate and visited—and danced!

But soon "rodeo" came to mean a tournament of cowboy (and cowgirl) skills, a cowboy circus or Olympics. One of the earliest Wild West stars was Annie Oakley, a world-famous sharpshooter. Although she couldn't even ride a horse when she first joined Buffalo Bill's Wild West Show in 1885, she impressed her co-star Chief Sitting Bull so much that he nicknamed her "Little Sure Shot." Later rodeo cowgirls rode (and fell off) bucking broncos, performed daring stunts on horseback, roped, and ran relays on racehorses.

Nowadays some cowgirl athletes compete in rodeo events such as bull and bronc riding. But most of them win their trophies, money, and fame as barrel racers, riding hard and fast on some of the most valuable horses in rodeo. Afterward these cowgirls still like to dance, but now they tap their toes and twirl to country and western instead of square dance music.